SHORTS

THAT GRAB ATTENTION!

40 Little Stories

By Robert S. Daley

SHORTS THAT GRAB ATTENTION! 40 LITTLE STORIES

ISBN: 97986 865931 (Paperback)

Contact the Aut ιr: robertsdaleyauthor@gmail.com

Dedication

Dedicated to my beautiful daughter, Emma.

And to all my family and friends.

Author's note

Writing this book was a bit like losing my virginity.

Once I found my rhythm, it was over in a flash.

Endorsement

The individual pieces are smart, pithy, biting little gems that had me chuckling and laughing out loud. I was so impressed I called my wife and read several to her.

You have a unique talent.

- Bill Pippin, Author of Wood Hick, Pigs-Ear, and Murphy.

Table of Content

A Story From A Handful Of Letters

My post-lady is always dressed in shorts – wet trousers would slow her down. Her lovely long legs bomb around the street. This morning, her van pulls up outside my ground-floor flat: *Shall I hang out the sheets? Do recycling? Deadhead the roses?* I drop my pen and grab the broom, head out to sweep up the leaves. She goes to 44, then skips up the steps to my block, carrying a handful of letters.

Morning John, somebody's popular, she says, handing me one. I don't look to see who it's from. As she walks back down the steps, whistling to herself, I head inside to finish another letter.

Pick Up

I had a friend I'd known since school named Chase, who never answered his phone. I'd leave long, meandering messages about my job, my girlfriend, the hot new secretary and what I ate for lunch. He'd tell me he was usually cooking when I called, either that or on the loo. I could visualise him, toilet paper in one hand, phone in the other. Faced with that dilemma, I wouldn't've expected him to take the call. I always answered the phone the minute he rang, like a penniless prostitute. One day, I let the phone ring. Three times he tried before he stopped calling. Weeks later, I found out he'd fallen off a ladder and died. The whole time I'd been thinking, when I saw him, I'd tell him I was throwing out the trash.

SHORTS THAT GRAB ATTENTION

The Meat Counter

I light the barbecue and place my jacket potato on the grill. I've just enough time to nip to my local supermarket to get the rest of the food. I walk at pace down the road, not stopping when Dot from No.32 sticks her head out the window and says *Where ye headin' off ta in such a hurry?*
I pick up some bits, glancing at my watch as I go. I get to the meat counter just before a heavily pregnant lady. There's one hamburger left... I salivate at the sight of it. But I let her go first.

For ten minutes, she asks for the butcher's opinion on the taste of the sage and onion sausages, as opposed to the Gloucester old spots, finally opting for the gourmet chipolatas; checks the price of a whole pork belly and a shank of lamb, and decides they are too expensive. When she asks how best to cook the brisket, I want the baby to kick her – hard.

I almost go to get a brioche bun, but somebody could take my place. So I put my hands on my hips and look at the ceiling.

Finally, she sticks the sausages in her trolley, wheels the front end away from the counter, and scans the meats one last time.

Just when I think it's mine, she says *Oh, and I'll take that burger too.*

The Girl On The Bus

The white girl throws her backpack up to the driver, who ties it onto the roof. The bus has stopped on the side of a road in Rajasthan, Northern India. The girl does the sign of the cross before she boards. She sits on the bumpy back seat. All the Indians turn and face her as if she's their entertainment for the journey. The bus drives on, dodging trucks and motorcycles and potholes. It is chaos! The girl covers her eyes, winces. The Indians are enjoying the show!

Scary Parts

Time to meet my Fred at Waterloo for a ride on the London Eye. It's our anniversary and he said it'd be a night to remember – he *better* propose. It's rush hour and everybody's waiting for the 5.42 at Edgware Road tube station. I met Fred, a general surgeon, three years ago straight out of Nursing College working at St. Thomas'. I should have gone up a band by now, but no one's retired lately and no one ever leaves. I'm tired of waiting. Waiting for the train, for a promotion, and most of all for Fred. If he doesn't come good now, he'll be *mince.*

An old man barges in front of me, stepping on my shoes, making my big toe throb. He's wearing grubby jeans and smells like the septic wound I dressed this morning. He stands behind a blonde lady, who'll be the first to board the train.

Bitch, he says, under his breath. The blonde hears.

Idiot, she mutters and looks at the tunnel. A gust of wind lifts a lock of hair over her ear as the haunting sound of the approaching train sends people shuffling forwards.

Everyone except the old man, who lifts his hands.

He grounds his right foot behind him, lets out a grunt and pushes the blonde over the edge. Arms and legs splayed like a skydiver, she lands face down on the tracks.

The train driver hits the brakes.

I've come across men like him in the hospital, broken and capable of heinous acts. I stride forwards and with all my might, shove him over the edge. The onlookers scream and cover their eyes, while inquisitive passengers press their faces to the train windows.

The train screeches past.

I imagine their bodies being torn to pieces, pieces even my Fred couldn't put back together. *What have I done? Would he still love me? Would he forgive me? Would he wait for me?* So many questions, when I was only expecting one.

Shopping Trip

I walk with my hands in the pockets of my ripped jeans, down the steps to my local supermarket. There's an iron railing running down the centre of the steps, but I keep my hands in my pockets. If I trip and fall, I want to look cool.

St. Ayla

They named St. Ayla after me, she once said. I didn't know why I'd stopped for the night here, likely some subconscious lure. I should have gotten the hell out of this Australian town soon as I'd arrived. Almost everything bore her name — shop signs, postcards, stamps, maps, even pet food. The memory of Ayla had spread through this place like a coronavirus.

The main street was a bustle of backpackers, aborigines, fortune-tellers, and priests. I spotted, fifty yards ahead, a dark female form with vibrant, tropical hair. Ayla moved in that same captivating way, like a drop of coffee smoothly running down the outside of a mug.

We'd parted in Byron Bay; I'd journeyed through the Outback to Uluru and was on my way home. *Could it be Ayla?* She drew closer, but I couldn't tell if she was the woman I'd betrayed. I wondered what I would say?

I hoped she'd stop right there, standing in the sunset's crimson glow, so the possibility remained that it was her. I pictured her face – it was like a beautiful constellation. But I'd see beyond that; to me, she was the black between the stars. Always just out of reach, she turned with the warm breeze and disappeared down a side street.

Dream Car

I drive a car I do *not* wish to be seen in. My Reliant Rialto is one reason people take buses. When traffic lights go green, drivers will put their foot down to avoid the indignity of being overtaken by my heap of crap. It's all I could afford at the time. I told myself when I get a job, I'd get something with four wheels. A 1.2 litre. Pale yellow or off-white, it doesn't matter. All I want is something people won't stop and stare at.

The Speed Date

My friend Paul had been single for seven years, so our other friend, Christine, suggested he go speed dating. Paul signed up and went to the Slug and Lettuce in Bristol one winter evening, to meet ten prospective partners. The way Paul tells it, it was a painful experience to start with. He found it difficult to engage in conversation with a stranger for five whole minutes. He kept asking the same questions over and over: *What do you do for a living? What are your hobbies? Who's your type?* and the women would ask him the same. Sometimes he'd sit in silence and seek inspiration from his glass of water as he struggled to think of anything to say.

But then he got to table 8, where he met Jamila from Senegal. They hit it off straight away. They were both thirty-eight and both wanted to get married and have kids. She laughed at his jokes, and he appreciated her wry sarcasm. They'd look into each others' eyes long after the conversation stopped. Paul was taken by her modest smile and her aura of tranquillity. *This is the one*, he thought. When the five minutes were up, they agreed to tick each other's boxes on their cards, for they seemed to be the perfect match.

When the results were released by the agency the next day, however, Paul found that Jamila hadn't ticked him as a match! Worse than that, he wouldn't be able to communicate with her via the app to find out why not. He'd gotten his hopes up, only for them to be dashed. Christine told him *That's the dating game for you!*

So, Paul went out and bought a Cockapoo. For months, he walked it along the Woodchester bike trail. He met a lot of dogs before he found Maria, his pregnant wife.

Mindfulness

I'm the only guy in the mindfulness class. We're all patients suffering from depression and anxiety and were referred by the psychiatrist.

Carol, the teacher, says *Just let your thoughts come and go in a non-judgmental way.*

Someone farts.

Filthy bitch, I think.

Roast, With All The Trimmings

Sara piles a slither of chicken, some stuffing, half a potato, a carrot and some cabbage onto her fork.

She says to Arnaldo: *Let's get married. I'll finish my drama course, then we'll have a baby. We'll live in that house you like, on the cliff overlooking the sea. You can teach me Italian.*

Arnaldo is open-mouthed as she fills her gob and delights in the combination of flavours.

The Scratchcard

It's 11 am – we're the first customers in the bar. We feel like shameful alcoholics, grateful when others arrive.

We're on our third pints when Tony notices a Mega Cashword scratchcard on the floor. *It probably belongs to him*, I say, pointing at a bearded man at the next table who looks like he frequents bookmakers, but Tony is insistent: *It's my favourite*, he says.

I reach over and scoop it up.

We'll go fifty-fifty, he says, taking a coin from his pocket. If we win a million, he'll say *he* saw it *first.*

As he scratches letters off the crossword, he bemoans the fact we don't have an N. If we had one of those, we would have won.

I think to myself: *Somebody must be kicking themselves, not knowing how much they didn't win.*

The Kite

Did Bella buy it for my birthday? Or did I buy it for hers? I think I bought that kite and it cost fifty pounds.

We took it to Minchinhampton Common on Sundays when the wind was up. We'd stand away from the other kite flyers – ours was a stunt kite. It would zoom through the air with a zipping sound, going this way and that, up and down, sometimes hanging in the same place, but not for long. We loved each other intensely when we flew that kite. It was exhilarating to feel in control of such a powerful thing, just for a while.

A Turbulent Night

I can't read my book. The girl upstairs has a boy round. Their bed is squeaking through the ceiling, distracting me.

I was glad when Yvonne moved in; she was single and the wrong side of pretty. I thought I'd never have to endure what I had to with the last tenants. Tomas and Mila, a German couple, would keep me up till the early hours with their humping and groaning.

But it's only taken Yvonne two weeks to find a willing mate. For me, it's been ten years. It annoys me when someone else is having sex in my vicinity and I'm not – I feel ridiculed.

But really, I just want to finish my story. It's about an aeroplane performing an emergency landing. Lydia Davis is a superb writer.

The Optical Illusion

The portly man on the next table in the beer garden was telling my mother and me a story about his boat.

He and his son were sailing off the Devon coast when their propellor got tangled with crab ropes. He said *I threw my son overboard with a knife,* though I suspect he didn't. In any case, his son failed to cut the propellor free, so they rode the tide until they were nestled on the beach sand. When the tide went out, leaving them stuck there, he, as the father, keen to display his superior nautical skills, got to work and soon accomplished what his son could not. With the job done and many hours to wait for the tide to come back in, they decided to go to the pub.

Meanwhile, a vessel came and towed their boat *The Optical Illusion* off the beach.

He and his son returned to find it gone. An observer told them it'd been taken away for salvage. *Hah!* the man said, supping his pint. He rubbed his fingers together and added *Cost me four grand to get it back.*

I felt he was trying to impress us. His eyes fixed on my mother, who peered into her coffee cup and scooped up some froth.

Nettles

Late for dinner at my sister's house, I hurry through the close. Bea's on the pavement ahead, tending to her shrubs. She's a looker and is well known around Painswick village for her many lovers. Her eight-year-old son, James, is with her.

As I pass, James says *Hello Roy* and shows off his flowerpot.

I've got nettles, he says, tilting the full pot towards me. Bea laughs. She's bent down with a trowel in her hand, peachy bum in the air.

She sits up, looks at me and says *Would you like to give me a hand? I could use a man with muscles.*

Hurrying past, I yell to James over my shoulder *Don't get stung!*

A Long (Way Down) Story

As Carl drove his mini down the rain-soaked street in Bath, he observed how his wipers moved in time to his music. Even when he stopped and started them again, they kept to the beat. This synchronicity intrigued him; maybe things were more ordered than he realised.

The cars in front pressed their brakes; a Jeep was indicating to pull into the car wash. Carl stopped. Suddenly, he spotted in his rear-view mirror a Range Rover travelling at high speed and not slowing down.

Instantly, Carl knew it was going to hit him. He felt the same sense of dread as he did when he inadvertently jumped off a bridge in Hamburg, thinking there was a road on the other side of the barrier – there wasn't. There was just a 200ft drop. If it wasn't for the scream of his friend, Aaron, he wouldn't have clung on at the last moment.

BANG!

His body slammed against his seat, his foot came off the brakes and his bumper shunted the car in front, causing him to be thrown into the steering wheel. Bruised, cut and slumped between life and death, Carl contemplated fatalism.

Proud Father

My wife and I were at the kindergarten for our daughter's initiation. The teacher asked Emma to take off her shoes, find her shoe-locker and put her shoes inside. Emma beamed confidently and picked up her pink canvas plimsolls. When I interjected with a helpful, *I think it's over there*, my wife grabbed my arm and gave me the eyes. *Dekiru-yo*, Emma announced and strutted off around the corner. She returned with *just* the *smuggest* look on her face. *Dekita!* she said. I turned to my wife and said *That girl can do anything!*

Teenagers

On my evening walk, I come across three girls sat the other side of the fence that runs along the path, on a ledge overlooking the canal. There's a fifty-foot drop to the water. They're playing hip hop music through a boom box. The loud girl has just palmed a pill to her friend. They don't notice me – teenagers are like starlings that only pay proper attention to other starlings. But I fear for their safety and urge to warn them of the danger as if they were *my* children. But then, my Katy and Sean never listened to a bloody word I said. So, I stand by the fence, keeping one eye on them whilst pretending to look at the bridge downstream. I hear one girl say *strange man*; the others look at me. My presence is making them feel uncomfortable, perhaps a little paranoid. Like a single black cloud covering the sun, I make no apology for being a nuisance. They jump over the fence, look at me thanklessly, and walk into town.

The Cold

Once, on a flight to Tenerife, the seat next to mine was empty. We'd just taken off when an attractive young brunette came and asked if she could sit in it. The passenger she'd been sitting next to had a nasty cold, she said. I had an awful cold myself, which had come on earlier that day, so I was most certainly contagious, but I didn't want to incur any more inconvenience upon such a lovely lady by making her find another seat, so I nodded and let her sit down. She gave me a soft smile.

Immediately, I felt a sneeze coming. I turned away from her, pinched my nose and held it in. A moment later, when I went to cough, I closed my mouth and squeezed my throat. I kept this up for four hours!

When we landed and got out of our seats, she thanked me. *Not at all,* I said.

Half-Cocked Boy

My girlfriend Leah and I were at a Libertines gig, stood near the stage. I was behind Leah, my arms wrapped around her tiny waist. Pete Doherty came out from the wings and positioned himself in front of his microphone. The heaving crowd erupted in wolf-whistles and screams. As the music started, a young lady jumped into my back and I felt her firm breasts, like horn bulbs, rubbing against me. She was unabashed and kept it up for the entire song, for the next song, and the one after that. I felt myself getting aroused, and Leah flicked me a devilish look to tell me she felt it too. The band played their last song and left the stage, and not knowing quite what else to do, I shouted *ENCORE!*

Chicken

Thirty-five years ago, I was in Cheltenham with my twelve-year-old friend Stefan, stood at a zebra crossing. The lights were on green and two lanes of heavy traffic rushed past. Stefan poked me on the arm and said *Watch this*, then ran straight out into the road, causing the drivers to brake and swerve as he skipped across the lanes. Once he'd made it to the other side, he yelled *COME ON* to me, beckoning me with a wave.

I didn't have it in me to risk my life like that. I'd barely survived premature birth and thought I shouldn't squander my existence so cheaply. So, I waited for the lights to go red and the cars to stop, then ambled across the road safely to join him.

CHICKEN! he yelled and flapped his arms. He thought he was clever.

Two years later, after he'd moved to Hong Kong, he was hit by a car whilst dodging traffic and died. They brought his body back to England for the funeral. The family said Stefan was *kind and well-mannered, the perfect son*, but I only remember him for his guts.

Buzz Off

I always leave the little top window in my lounge open. The place needs to be kept aired otherwise damp will form. Occasionally a fly will enter through the window and buzz about my head whilst I am typing. So, I open the large window in the hope that it will leave. More usually, another fly will come into the room through this larger window. Now I have two flies annoying me. So, I go to the front door and open it wide as *if* they'd get the hint.

Distant Relative

My half-Japanese daughter, Emma, rings from five thousand miles away.

Phone lodged between shoulder and ear, I take her framed photograph off the window ledge and study her chocolatey eyes. *She was six then*, I muse as she harps on about university entrance exams and her new Honda Ballade.

I wipe the dust off the glass with my sleeve.

Sayonara daddy, she says – it startles me.

Hold on, I say, sitting forwards, but she's already gone.

Friday Street, London

The white-van-man is punching somebody through their open car window. Nobody else on the street is doing anything about this, so I run to help. I should wonder: *Why am I sacrificing myself for a stranger? Is it the instinct to do the right thing, or perhaps the invincibility of youth?* The victim might be a dog abuser, a homophobe or a racist, in which case they'd deserve a beating. But I keep running. Mid-stride I shout *STOP THAT!* as threateningly as I can. The thug gets back in his van and drives off. I peer into the car – an ashen-faced old man is shaking all over. I softly touch his shoulder. A driver, five cars back, honks his horn.

Change Jar

When my change jar is nearly full, but not so full it's too heavy to carry, I'll take it to the machine in my local supermarket to convert the coins into notes. I can't stand carrying loose change; when I put my hands in my *pockets*, I like my fingers to be comfortable, so I add to my jar whenever the opportunity arises. At some point, I must have been content to carry coins, for I wouldn't have brought them back from Nepal, Japan and Australia if I was not, but I do not remember when or why this changed. Normally, I'll use my debit card for my groceries but my Aunty will often send me some cash and rather than endure the long queue at the bank, where there's just a single teller, which infuriates me no end, I'll spend it. But it's difficult to spend twenty pounds exactly, so invariably I'll be left with some change in my pockets. When I empty my jar through the slot in the machine, the coins seem to drop into an abyss; strangely, there are no clinking sounds from within. The foreign coins, however, are regurgitated into the change slot. They each hold memories of jagged mountains and swirling rapids, cherry blossoms and red rocks – memories I can't leave behind. So, once more, into my jar they go, to come back to me at a later date.

Spun Out

One night, I was playing blackjack with my friend, Raymond, at the Grosvenor Casino. He noticed that one of the roulette tables was showing a streak of twenty blacks in a row. So, he left the blackjack table and rushed over. I followed him. He liked to throw his money about when the urge took him, so he promptly placed a £100 bet on red.

The ball landed on 15 black.

I took it upon myself to be the voice of reason, suggesting to him that streaks meant nothing; there was always a 47.4% chance of being right when betting red or black, no matter what had gone on before. He threw me a scathing look as if to say *Don't be absurd!*

He doubled his bet, on red again. *You watch, it's gonna come in now,* he said.

The croupier spun the wheel. This time, the ball hit 28 black.

At this rate, the only red number Raymond would see would be on his bank balance.

He doubled his bet again. He was now risking £400 on red. His eyes were twitching, his fingers picking at his cuticles. Others had joined in and there was a huge stack of notes and chips on the red square.

Again, it came in black. Everyone groaned. Raymond had busted out. *That's friggin' rotten luck,* he said. He'd just lost his month's salary; his wife wouldn't be happy. I could understand the attraction for it was extremely exciting, but I'd rather spend the money on a two-week holiday in Greece.

I went back to the blackjack table and played a few more one-pound hands, while Raymond stood by the Roulette table, waiting for the red to come in. Two spins later, both blacks, I spotted him hawking his gold ring.

Dating App Profiles

Yazz 33

An enigma wrapped up in a riddle....no drama, no baggage, no hook-ups.

Lorna 38

Here for polite conversation and romantic dates! I may be in the wrong place. Restore my faith in men.

Tammie 42

Fuckboys need not apply.

Tina 40

I am 40, have 3 children. I love movies and theatre and nice meals with nice wine. I don't go out on the pull anymore, so let's see how this goes.

Mary 36

I'm an animal lover.

Bex 37

Mummy to a little girl and a little dog and both are my

world.

Gemma 45

Gym-lover. Make a banging cup of tea.

Kim 44

r u out there? You must like cats. I don't want to d8 any1 with kids.

Sharon 47

Funky, chunky girl recently discovered a love for pilates and healthy living.

Georgina 35

Wanna chat? Bla bla bla.

Sarah 31

Interested in dad bods or someone who works out occasionally. If your nips are out on your photo, then no. Put them away!

Kylie 41

Looking for someone to protect me from spiders.

Katy 38

I like someone who has something about

them…preferably not strange.

Theresa 43

Funny bit mad sometimes but who wants boring.

Marianne 36

If you're a fan of fish lips or feather duster eyelashes or one-night stands, please move along. Looking to date, not chat.

Diana 44

Been single for about 100 years now! Apply within.

Karen 32

Recently active.

Nicola 34

377 kilometres away.

The Fatphobe

Fat fat fat. That's all granny Joy thinks about. Anyone would think I'm overweight. Well, I am a little bit, but that's not the point. She's obsessed with it! *You must stop eating greasy foods and eat more vegetables*, she'll say. *Do you want diabetes?* What sort of question is that? God forbid I tell her what I had for tea last night – I had a hot chicken tikka masala ready meal and two large naans washed down with a can of Guinness. I can hear her now calculating the calories in her head, which is set on self-destruct.

When I'm with her, and she sees a particularly obese person in the street, she'll say *Is that how you want to end up?* She's an unadulterated fatphobe. She acts like I'm double my weight – I'm 11 stone. The whole family is affected, not just me. I find it counter-productive – the more she goes on about fat, the more fat I want to eat. She should have cottoned on to this by now. There's only thing to do – find myself a fiery, plump, Sicilian girlfriend just to stir things up.

Trade War

Two Americans, lovers, had gone missing the day before. They'd been swimming upstream in the Mekong River in Si Phan Don. Our hostel owner, Tho, reckoned the electric eels had got them and they'd have floated right past our huts overnight. The thought of dead bodies eerily making their way downstream as we slept was sure to give me nightmares. Word came from across the Cambodian border that a fisherman had discovered the male body. The female was still missing. A group of fishermen, gathered by our huts, wanted me to negotiate a fee with the police for the return of the body on behalf of the Cambodian fisherman. I was reluctant, for I wasn't sure what an American was worth these *days*. They told me the police were offering a reward of five million kip, but the fisherman wanted ten. I told them he should find the woman then. But they were insistent, the body would not be delivered unless his asking price was met. The police weren't going to budge either. I thought of the family back in the States, watching the news and waiting by their phones while their relative was caught up in a trade war where no one wins.

The Confession

She'd spent most of her teenage years in bed, suffering from chronic fatigue syndrome; had just started to get out of the house. He'd met her at the library, watched her leaf through books, skipping through chapters. They'd talk about all the things she'd do, all the journeys she'd take to the coasts and the hills. He'd help her reconnect with life.

One night, after drinks at her local Botanist bar, he stayed over, on her couch. He lay awake till two in the morning, wondering if she was lying awake too. He put on his T-shirt and slacks and went to her room. She was asleep. Moonlight pooled in through the gap in the curtains and lit up the side of her face so it looked like a planet – it had a gravitational pull. He sat on her little sofa and coughed softly, and when she didn't wake he coughed louder and said a little too sternly, *Evie.*

She woke from her slumber, rubbing her eyes. *What is it?* He cleared his throat, readying himself. *I've got something to tell you.* She lifted a lock of hair from her face. He said *I like you more than a friend.* She looked sideways at the wall and scratched her nose. Lifted herself onto her elbows. *I'm sorry Jake...I um...don't see you that way.* Her turndown hit him like a boot to the face. He ran down the stairs and bolted out the front door.

He strode through the streets, his tears mingling with rain droplets, bringing an unexpected sense of newness. On Clifton Avenue, under a globe street lamp and surrounded by shimmering puddles of light, he stood for a while to get his bearings. A taxi pulled up. The driver asked him where he was going. Jake answered *Asia.*

Getting Through Immigration

The crazy Chinese immigration official points a gun in my face. He screams sharp *XIs* and *ZAOs* as if arguing with himself, and not understanding a word he's saying, I look desperately at the meek young lady sitting next to him. She sheepishly lifts the brim of her hat. It's then I realise the officer wants me to take off my cap. So, I do. After all, he has a gun in my face.

The Subplot

When I go to the cinema with my sister, Roxie, she'll insist we sit in the central VIP seats, even though we bought cheap seats. When the rightful owners come to claim their seats, which they invariably do, she'll say indignantly *Someone took ours, so we're sitting here.* The irritated patrons, loath to make a fuss, will find alternative seats at the end of the row. As the film starts, Roxie will take off her shoes and put her feet up on the chair in front and munch open-mouthed on her popcorn, shaking her carton so it sounds like a rattle. She knows her poor etiquette makes me feel uncomfortable – it's part of her enjoyment. If I show my displeasure, it simply encourages her. When the tension builds in a suspenseful scene, she'll wait for that deathly quiet moment when everyone is hanging on the next word, then take a long, gurgled slurp of her Coke. She could care less about the shushes. She'll go to the toilet two, sometimes three times, using her mobile's flashlight to navigate her way down the steps as she goes out and up the steps as she comes back. At the end of the film, she'll ask me what I thought of it, and I'll nod approvingly, not wanting her to know how much I hated it.

The Upper Hand

There was a particular moment in my relationship when my girlfriend first got the upper hand. It wasn't that yawn when I was speaking, or when she talked over me on that couples' date, or even when she yelled *You left the butter out of the fridge again!* Nor was it the day she bought a lacy red chemise and a vibrator that was bigger than my thingy. No, it was way before then – it was that moment in our very first kiss when my tongue tired of the fight for supremacy and, verging on suffocation, I stopped for air.

The Stricken Man

The man was out where the waves were breaking, waving his arms. The seas were choppy around Durdle Door and swimmers often got into difficulty. The beachgoers, sensing something was wrong, gathered in a group, twenty strong. One by one, they stepped out into the sea – their linked arms forming a human chain – until they reached the stricken man. A wave threw him into the arms of Peter, the nearest rescuer – the man clung on like a baby monkey. Then they all pulled him back to the safety of the shore. The coastguard praised the efforts of the public, saying *had it not been for their actions, the outcome could have been very different.* On hearing these words, the rescuers felt an enormous sense of pride. Peter was so inspired by this praise that he applied for a job with the Maritime and Coastguard Agency. He worked for them for twenty years and saved countless lives, but the story he always told his grandchildren was the one that happened at Durdle Door.

The Quick Thief, The Old Lady And The Slow Man

Right in front of me, the scruffy young man attacked the old lady. He put his hand in her face and ripped her handbag from her as she fell to the ground. Then he made off up the High Street. I was beset by this dilemma: *Do I give chase or do I help the old lady?* I wasn't entirely sure what the correct protocol was? What would the old lady want me to do? Did she care more for the contents of her purse or the fact her drawers were showing? I dithered, and by the time I'd made my mind up to first help the old lady, others had stepped in, and by that point, the thief was gone. The old lady was on her feet now. I wanted it to look like I'd done something, so I ran a few yards, stopped and flung my arms in the air.

Mania

You become impatient with the world around you because even police cars responding to emergencies move so goddamn slowly. You're five steps ahead of everyone else, especially your distinguished and wholly exasperated psychiatrist, Dr R J Blacker. Touched by God, no less, you're in a constant state of spiritual awakening – you invite Jehovah Witnesses to your home to discuss the end of days over tea and biscuits. You donate your benefits to charity and stop killing spiders. On strolls through the country lanes, you walk wherever the wind takes you. Keen to do your bit for the global water shortage, you collect the drops from your dripping tap. You write lengthy, illegible letters to the council complaining about the demons in your attic, telling them in no uncertain terms that their inaction is making you so very, very mad.

Depression

There are no words to describe the horror. The anguish is so great and time goes so agonizingly slowly, you just want it all to end. *Surely death is preferable*, you think. *But how can you know?* Sue, my nurse astutely asked. I could tell you it's like flying in a Cessna jet through the thick black cloud in the Himalayas. Petrified, you stare hopelessly at the foggy windows while the pilots press buttons, look quizzically at each other, and press more buttons. Your companion tries to reassure you but you feel utterly helpless. In a sense, of course, you've already crashed. Somewhere south of Machupuchare.

Call Me Roberto

As you know by now, my name is Robert, or Rob for short. Standing at 5ft 3", I should have a short name.

ROBERT! is reserved for my crabby grandmother, who castigates me when we're making gnocchi and I drop one on the floor.

My mum calls me Bobby, and my dad, brother and sister – Bobs.

Bobby was what I used in Japan when I taught English to elementary school children. The Japanese can't pronounce their Rs correctly; they say *Lobert.* So, I called myself Bobby, for their sake, and I suppose mine.

My Japanese ex-wife still calls me Bobby; my other exes call me all sorts of names.

My school friends used to call me Dales; the bullies – monster and egghead.

The Italian signora, stood in the window overlooking Specchio piazza, wearing only a bath towel, offered a seductive 'Rober*to.*'

That I liked.

I wasn't so enamoured by the Japanese nympho who had a thing for footballers; she screamed an orgasmic

'*ROBERTO BAGGIO!*' in my ear!

I told her: *Call me Roberto.*

The Trader

In 2010, I thought I should find an alternative income to my teaching. I was mindful of my health issues and needed security in case I couldn't work my day job. I had a family to provide for, after all. So, I bought an online forex trading course and downloaded a platform. *I was going to make it rich,* I thought.

I lost five grand in the first week.

But I did better after that – took me ten years to lose the next five grand. Then I quit and wrote this book.

Acknowledgements

Thanks to Lara and Alex, for reading my dodgy drafts and being gracious in their feedback, and to Bill Pippin, Eli Joseph, S. M. Savoy and all the other contributors at Scribophile.

About The Author

Robert S. Daley is a mental health nurse living in Stroud UK. He has spent most of his life in England but has also lived in Hong Kong, Japan and Australia, and travelled extensively throughout South-East Asia. This book of short stories represents his first serious attempt to create a lasting piece of work.

If you enjoyed this book, please leave a review at Amazon.com

Links

You can find his website at www.robertsdaley.com, his blog at www.robertsdaley.blogspot.com and his Facebook page at www.facebook.com/RobertSDaleyStroud

Printed in Great Britain
by Amazon

59849425R10058